Samuel French Acting

MW00773244

Five Mile Lake

by Rachel Bonds

SAMUELFRENCH.COM   SAMUELFRENCH.CO.UK

FOR PRODUCTION ENQUIRIES

UNITED STATES AND CANADA
Info@SamuelFrench.com
1-866-598-8449

UNITED KINGDOM AND EUROPE
Plays@SamuelFrench.co.uk
020-7255-4302

Each title is subject to availability from Samuel French, depending
upon country of performance. Please be aware that *FIVE MILE LAKE*
may not be licensed by Samuel French in your territory. Professional
and amateur producers should contact the nearest Samuel French
office or licensing partner to verify availability.

MUSIC USE NOTE

IMPORTANT BILLING AND CREDIT REQUIREMENTS

FIVE MILE LAKE was originally produced by South Coast Repertory in Costa Mesa, California in April of 2014. The performance was directed by Daniella Topol, with scenic design by Marion Williams, costume design by David Kay Mickelson, lighting design by Lap Chi Chu, and sound design by composer Vincent Olivieri. The Stage Manager was Jennifer Ellen Butler. The cast was as follows:

JAMIE ....Nate Mooney
MARY ....Rebecca Mozo
RUFUS..Corey Brill
PETA..Nicole Shalhoub
DANNY.. Brian Slaten

FIVE MILE LAKE was subsequently produced by McCarter Theatre Center in Princeton, New Jersey (Emily Mann, Artistic Director; Timothy J. Shields, Managing Director) in May of 2015. The performance was directed by Emily Mann, with set design by Edward Pierce, costume design by Jennifer von Mayrhauser, lighting design by Jeff Croiter, and original music and sound design by Daniel Perelstein. The Production Stage Manager was Cheryl Mintz. The cast was as follows:

JAMIE .... Tobias Segal
MARY ....Kristen Bush
RUFUS... Nathan Darrow
PETA..Mahira Kakkar
DANNY...Jason Babinsky

CHARACTERS

JAMIE

MARY

RUFUS

PETA*

DANNY

*Author's Note: Peta was originally written for a South Asian actor, though we cast an actor of Middle Eastern descent in the world premiere production, and this casting also made sense.

SETTING

A small, somewhat desolate town near Scranton, PA. By a lake.

TIME

Winter.

AUTHOR'S NOTES

A slash (/) indicates where the next line should begin. For instance:

RUFUS. We're not engaged.

JAMIE. What? / That's –

RUFUS. That's what you were going to ask, right?

1. The Bakery

*(Early morning. The bakery. **MARY** and **JAMIE** set up: He prepares coffee and sets up the coffee station; she arranges the bakery case. She is in a dark cloud, very drawn into herself. He observes her as they work quietly.)*

MARY. Can you hand me that?

JAMIE. *(Handing her a box of baked goods.)* Yeah – / sure.

MARY. That one too.

JAMIE. *(Handing her another box.)* Yeah – yup.

(She takes the boxes from him without looking at him and works quickly, clouded. He puzzles at her.)

...What's up with you?

MARY. What?

JAMIE. You seem, / like –

MARY. What?

JAMIE. You're all, like...

(He does some brief imitation of her going through her tasks robotically, shell-shocked.)

MARY. I'm fine.

JAMIE. Okay.

MARY. Okay...

(She turns back to her task, annoyed.)

JAMIE. ...Did you watch any hockey last night?

MARY. I hate hockey.

JAMIE. *No* – but this is – this isn't like normal hockey, this is like –

MARY. I don't like hockey.

JAMIE. But THIS hockey is like when everyone plays AGAINST their own teammates and / it's crazy.

MARY. Don't like hockey.

JAMIE. But this is – you'll like this. They tell everyone's family back-stories and you get all personally involved with all / of them...

MARY. They're all such dicks, though. They all get such pleasure out of beating each other up.

JAMIE. That's just – part of / the game.

MARY. Would you ever want to hang out with a hockey player though? They're probably all really mean and aggressive and like / drunk all the time –

JAMIE. Fine, okay – but they're fun to watch. They're really good at what they do and that's Fun To Watch. You don't have to hang out with / them.

MARY. I / know that.

JAMIE. Okay, so –... You've been watching figure skating?

MARY. I'm not talking to you about it.

JAMIE. Have you?

MARY. It's a sport, / Jamie.

JAMIE. Yeahhh, not really / a sport.

MARY. It's a / sport.

JAMIE. Not really a sport, / Mary.

MARY. Have you seen the legs on those people? Their muscles are like bulging out all over the – they are serious athletes, Jamie.

JAMIE. I don't know if they're *serious* / athletes...

MARY. JAMIE STOP.

JAMIE. Okay!

    (Quiet.)

I mean they wear glittery costumes.

MARY. Seriously – fuck off.

JAMIE. Whoa!

MARY. Just – I said I wasn't talking about it.

JAMIE. Sorry.

> *(They work silently for a moment. She grabs a bag of cat food hidden under a shelf and heads outside.)*

You know if you keep feeding them they're going to multiply.

MARY. Then I'll get more food.

JAMIE. I don't know if it's a good thing to do.

MARY. What else are they going to eat?

JAMIE. Birds. Moles. Wild things. They hunt, Mary.

MARY. They're hungry.

JAMIE. But what if they become dependent on you and forget how to fend for themselves?

> *(She gives him a look and turns to go outside.)*

Okay, feed them – But don't be surprised if you go out there one day and there's like forty cats sitting there waiting for you.

MARY. I would love that.

JAMIE. Like, "Feeeeeeeeed ussssssss."

MARY. If I get locked out, let me / back in.

JAMIE. "Marryyyyyy, feeeed usss."

MARY. Goodbye.

> *(She disappears into the back.* **JAMIE** *stares after her, then goes back to arranging the coffee station.)*

> *(***MARY*** *re-enters.)*

JAMIE. How were they?

MARY. Hungry.

JAMIE. Yup.

MARY. You know you like them.

JAMIE. Euhhh... They're kind of crazy looking.

MARY. What?

JAMIE. I mean – they look kind of rabid / or something.

MARY. They're stray cats, they're not – going to look like the Fancy Feast commercial / or whatever.

JAMIE. I know.

MARY. You know if I weren't here you'd be back there feeding them out of your hand.

JAMIE. *(Cringing.)* Errr – doubtful.

MARY. Okay, fine, you'll let them starve and freeze to death.

> *(She goes back to work, quiet. They are silent for several moments.)*

JAMIE. Hey – how's Danny doing?

MARY. *(Not looking up.)* Danny's fine.

JAMIE. You know there's this incentive thing where businesses get a bonus from the government if they hire him.

MARY. We know.

JAMIE. So, but – he hasn't found anything / yet?

MARY. Not yet.

JAMIE. Okay. Well… I don't know, if he wants, maybe I could talk to some people for him, ask around…

MARY. Yeah, maybe…

JAMIE. I mean, it must be hard, / like –

MARY. Yup.

JAMIE. It must be really hard to…have such a serious purpose, and like, sense of duty and everything, and then have that disappear completely.

MARY. Yeah.

JAMIE. Especially for Danny, he's so… He seems to need that – sense of purpose thing. Anyway.

> *(**MARY** studies a spot on the counter, rubbing it with a cloth. **JAMIE** goes back to his task. **MARY** rubs the spot on the counter. Several moments pass.)*

MARY. …So were you on that email?

JAMIE. What email?

MARY. That Jared sent about getting married?

JAMIE. Oooh, yeah. I was. On that.

MARY. Yeahhh.

JAMIE. I thought it was weird he sent a mass email.

MARY. Me too.

JAMIE. He didn't...tell you before or / anything?

MARY. Nope.

JAMIE. Are you pissed?

MARY. Pissed? Not really.

JAMIE. But you're...

MARY. I don't know.

JAMIE. Sad?

MARY. No.

JAMIE. Melancholy?

MARY. *(Laughing.)* "Melancholy?" Yeah – maybe.

JAMIE. Why though? You're always saying how much of a dick / he was.

MARY. Well, yeah, he's completely – emotionally incapable, but...I don't know, I'm still just kind of HERE, like – treading water – and he's going off to really live his stupid life somewhere.

JAMIE. Yeah, in Philadelphia. It's not like the – like Paris.

MARY. *(Shrugging.)* Still.

Don't you ever get claustrophobic? – Like don't you ever want to just tear your skin off and run away and be a whole different person?

JAMIE. No. Because I live on a huge lake.

MARY. *(Rolling her eyes.)* Oh god.

JAMIE. ...So I can go outside and stare out at the huge, beautiful lake every day...and that feels very un-claustrophobic.

MARY. But Jamie, it's a lake.

JAMIE. So?

MARY. So it's finite and man-made.

JAMIE. I know.

MARY. And shallow and muddy / and –

JAMIE. I like my / lake.

MARY. – Too small to contain anything interesting.

JAMIE. Jesus – well it's big enough for me.

MARY. Well we are very different people.

JAMIE. ...I guess. What, you want to go live in Philly?

MARY. Maybe, I don't know. Or New York.

JAMIE. Eugh, New York is nasty.

MARY. It's not – why is it *nasty*?

JAMIE. There's people just, like, in your face, all the time, and – trash, like, all over the street – seriously, the last time I was there it was everywhere, and we were in this place in...I think, like, Chinatown, and there was this nasty / *smell* –

MARY. Well yeah, it's a city.

JAMIE. People seriously, like, take shits on the street. / On the street.

MARY. *(Rolling her eyes.)* Oh god.

JAMIE. They do.

MARY. Okay – well. It's a city, Jamie. People do all kinds of things.

> (**JAMIE** *climbs on the counter and begins writing the names of muffins, specials, etc. on the chalkboard menu.*)

JAMIE. Today's cranberry walnut, right?

MARY. Yeah.

God – Jared's such a dick. "Just wanted to share the good news...!"

JAMIE. *(Writing carefully.)* He's just excited.

MARY. He's a dick.

JAMIE. Yeah. My ex-girlfriend's married.

MARY. But Melissa's your high school girlfriend.

JAMIE. So?

MARY. So you high-school-loved her. I adult-loved Jared.

JAMIE. It was still weird when she got married.

MARY. She is ALWAYS tapping her ring against the counter.

JAMIE. *(Jumping down from the counter.)* What?

MARY. She doesn't do this to you? When Melissa comes in, she always stares into the bakery case and pretends to be thinking really hard about what she wants and she taps her little ring finger against the glass like TAP TAP TAP, MAN, I canNOT decide WHAT BAKERY ITEM I WANT to BUY toDAY, and OH MY GOD, LOOK HOW HUGE MY DIAMOND RING IS.

JAMIE. It is huge, isn't it?

MARY. It's ridiculous.

JAMIE. Like kind of gawdy, right?

MARY. YES. I would never wear that.

JAMIE. Yeah, good, I would never buy that. For / anyone.

> *(A loud knock on the glass interrupts them.* **JAMIE** *and* **MARY** *jump and look out toward the noise.* **RUFUS** *and* **PETA** *stand outside;* **RUFUS** *pounds on the glass.)*

(Squinting.) ...Rufus? Oh my god, what the...

> *(**JAMIE** lets them in. **MARY** smooths her hair.)*
> *(**RUFUS** and **PETA** step inside.)*

RUFUS. Hey are you open yet? We're starving, feed us.

JAMIE. Rufus, what the? What are you –

> *(They hug.)*

It's been / forever.

RUFUS. I know.

JAMIE. What the hell are you doing here?

RUFUS. You know... Oh, sorry – this is Peta.

JAMIE. *(Offering his hand.)* Peta. Hey – I'm Jamie.

PETA. *(Shaking his hand.)* Hi. It's so nice to meet you.

JAMIE. Yeah, um – it's nice to meet you too.

PETA. *(Smiling politely.)* I've heard a lot about you.

JAMIE. Oh – well, that's – thanks, that's – god, sorry, I'm just – I did NOT expect to see YOU / today.

RUFUS. I know, it's kind of crazy.

JAMIE. What time did you leave the city?

RUFUS. Uhhh...early.

JAMIE. Yeah, seriously. What's going on?

RUFUS. Uhh, nothing, really, we just...decided to take a little trip.

JAMIE. Cool, okay. Oh, sorry – you remember Mary?

RUFUS. Uh – yeah – hey Mary.

MARY. Hi.

RUFUS. Danny's sister.

MARY. Right.

RUFUS. *(To* **PETA.***)* Danny was a friend of mine in high school.

PETA. Ahh, nice.

RUFUS. Peta, Mary.

PETA. Hello.

MARY. Hi.

JAMIE. Seriously, though, are you guys – what are your plans, are you just driving through?

RUFUS. No, we came for a visit.

JAMIE. Okay. Okay, awesome.

RUFUS. Thought we'd take some time, stare at the water, relax, you know... Is that okay?

JAMIE. Yeah! – Yeah totally.

RUFUS. Good. Okay.

JAMIE. Um...well, welcome home.

RUFUS. Thanks.

(They all stand quietly.)

2. The Backyard

(Late night. **JAMIE** *and* **RUFUS** *behind the lake house. They sit at a picnic table. They share a bottle of whiskey. Though it's cold, they've stopped noticing.)*

RUFUS. So then *he* – *he* then tries to *recover* and pretends that he DIDN'T say what he just said, like tries to coast over it *entirely* – and she's standing there with like, mouth agape, like – "What the fuuuuuuck did you just say?" – and he's like fumbling around saying like, "Well anyway what I meant was, see what I'm trying to say is blah blah," and while he's like shitting his pants she just like – ohmygod – she just *rears back* and – *(He gestures a sucker punch.)* WHAM! – she just punches the guy right / in the face.

JAMIE. *(Laughing.)* Ohmygod.

RUFUS. I KNOW! And then like the whole room goes quiet and he's clutching his face and making this *weird* whimpering sound and everyone's staring at him, except for me – because I'm looking at *her* – and you can barely see it, like it's barely there, it's just this tiny, tiny, tiny thing, but I see it. She has this subtle, little snarl going / on – like –

JAMIE. A snarl?

RUFUS. Yes! Like her lip is slightly curved up on one side – it's really small, like almost imperceptible – but it's there – this like real *animal* thing. And that's it, then I'm just like, "I must know this girl. This girl must be in my daily life from now on." Just... I mean she really beat the shit out of him. And then that little *snarl*. How do you not walk across the room and immediately introduce yourself to that girl?

JAMIE. I don't know.

RUFUS. So.

JAMIE. That's crazy.

RUFUS. I know! God.

Oh shit – it's late. Do you have to be at work in like four hours? I don't want you to get fired.

JAMIE. No, it's okay – I'm basically managing this location now, so.

RUFUS. Nice.

JAMIE. Yeah – Brad's mostly out at the Waynesboro location so he's never around. And I know he won't come in tomorrow. Er, well, today. Shit.

RUFUS. That's cool.

JAMIE. Yeah.

RUFUS. *(Drinking.)* God this tastes good.

JAMIE. I know.

RUFUS. Everything tastes better when you're outside.

JAMIE. And you're staring at a lake.

RUFUS. And it's negative degrees. Cheers.

    (They drink.)

JAMIE. So…

RUFUS. We're not engaged.

JAMIE. What? / That's –

RUFUS. That's what you were going to ask, right?

JAMIE. NO. I was not.

RUFUS. What were you going to ask?

JAMIE. I was going to ask what your plans are.

RUFUS. Uhhh…

JAMIE. Like how long are you staying?

RUFUS. I don't know, a few days?

JAMIE. Okay.

RUFUS. We just need a little time off from everything.

JAMIE. Like what?

RUFUS. Just – everything. Work. I've been totally consumed by my dissertation lately.

JAMIE. Right.

RUFUS. And Peta's been working like mad, so –

JAMIE. Cool. Okay, well – it's awesome you're here. It's seriously been forever.

RUFUS. Yeah yeah, I know.

I mean, to be perfectly honest...

JAMIE. What?

RUFUS. I actually didn't know you'd be here.

JAMIE. I live here.

RUFUS. I know that, yes.

JAMIE. ...Sooo?

RUFUS. I mean I knew you'd be in town and we'd see you, I just didn't know you'd be *here* here – in the lake house.

JAMIE. Mom didn't tell you?

RUFUS. I don't know, maybe she did?

JAMIE. I've been fixing it up like crazy over the past year.

RUFUS. Maybe I knew and I forgot...? I don't know.

JAMIE. Well...sorry dude. Did I ruin your romantic getaway or / something?

RUFUS. No no, that's not what I meant. It was just a surprise.

JAMIE. Right.

RUFUS. No, it's good. You get to really meet Peta this way.

JAMIE. Yeahhh. You gotta drive her out to meet Mom.

RUFUS. Yeah, yeah – We don't have a ton of time off, but, / yeah...

JAMIE. Because she is always asking me if I've spoken to you, which I haven't – and then we spend like an hour talking about why you haven't called her...

RUFUS. Shit, sorry. I've been so distracted with writing / and –

JAMIE. I know.

RUFUS. My brain's just been elsewhere, you know?

JAMIE. Yeah. So – wait, your...thing – your dissertation – what's it about?

RUFUS. Oh god. Uhhh – You'll think it's boring.

JAMIE. No I won't.

RUFUS. I mean I don't know if it'll mean anything to you.

JAMIE. Come onnn.

RUFUS. Uhhhh, okay. Okay. So – it's about mourning. Well, more specifically, it's about laments.

JAMIE. Laments.

RUFUS. Yeah – the laments for the dead. In Greek tragedy. And in the *Iliad*.

JAMIE. We read that! In tenth grade!

RUFUS. Yeah, probably. So, okay, it's about communal laments – which were almost always led by women, because they were basically professional mourners, performing these like impassioned rituals – like when Hector dies in the *Iliad*, right – the line goes: "They put him on a carved bed, and stood singers beside him, leaders of laments, who lamented in grievous song, and the women wailed. And the white-armed Andromache began their wailing." – I love that image of her being "white-armed."

JAMIE. Yeah.

RUFUS. So – right, but it's also about characters individually protesting against death. Like when Patroclus is killed – Achilles has this amazingly intense moment – his weeping is SO LOUD, that Thetis, his mother, who's down being a nymph in the DEPTHS of the SEA, can hear it. And then he goes like wild with grief and covers himself in ash and starts tearing out his hair... it's wonderfully dramatic stuff. Women wailing and beating their breasts and hair getting torn out of people's heads and just... It's fantastic.

JAMIE. Whoa.

RUFUS. So.

JAMIE. Cool. That means something to me.

RUFUS. Okay, good – I didn't know...

JAMIE. That's intense stuff.

RUFUS. God, yes – everything that everyone feels is incredibly vast and epic and and...it's just so much better than real life, you know?

JAMIE. Right, yeah. So how long is it?

RUFUS. Uhhhh god... I don't know, a million pages?

JAMIE. I mean, how much have you written?

RUFUS. Definitely over a hundred pages at this / point.

JAMIE. Jesus. You've written a hundred pages of something?

RUFUS. Yeah.

JAMIE. That's crazy.

RUFUS. And it's not done.

JAMIE. How long's it going to be?

RUFUS. Two hundred something, I / imagine.

JAMIE. JESUS.

RUFUS. Yup.

JAMIE. That's insane. TWO HUNDRED PAGES – that's like a *book*.

RUFUS. I know.

JAMIE. Shit. Cheers.

RUFUS. Cheers.

   (They drink.)

So, hey – what's with Mary?

JAMIE. Mary? Nothing.

RUFUS. Nothing.

JAMIE. Nothing.

RUFUS. Really.

JAMIE. Yes. Unfortunately.

RUFUS. Haaaa YES, I KNEW IT!

JAMIE. What?!

RUFUS. I thought so.

JAMIE. There's nothing going on.

RUFUS. Why not?

JAMIE. Because. She's – she's got a lot of other stuff... happening.

RUFUS. Like what?

JAMIE. Well, like Danny just moved back in with her a couple months / ago.

RUFUS. Okay...

JAMIE. And he did two tours.

RUFUS. Whoa.

JAMIE. – In Afghanistan. And... He's having a hard time finding work, / so...

RUFUS. Ah.

JAMIE. So, she has a lot to deal with and I don't know, she doesn't need people – me – bugging her.

RUFUS. Bugging her.

JAMIE. I don't know! – But also she's so freaking beautiful I don't know what to do.

RUFUS. Yeahhhh – wasn't she a track star or something?

JAMIE. Cross-country.

RUFUS. Yeah – I remember that. She was good, right?

JAMIE. Yeah. She was.

RUFUS. Yeah yeah... I feel like – yeah, I remember seeing her – like I'd be driving home late and she'd always be out running on Brakefield Road? And she was like this – thing, this – like this mystical creature racing down the streets in the middle of the night.

JAMIE. Sounds like her.

RUFUS. Just tell her she's a mystical nighttime creature.

JAMIE. Yeahhh, I'm not good at saying things like that.

RUFUS. Women love being told they're mystical.

JAMIE. I'm sure they do. It just sounds retarded when I say something like that.

RUFUS. Just try it.

JAMIE. Great, I'll go in tomorrow and tell her she's a creature.

RUFUS. A mystical nighttime creature.

JAMIE. Perfect.

> *(They drink.)*

So, um...what do you think?

RUFUS. About...

JAMIE. The house.

RUFUS. Ohhh – It looks good.

JAMIE. Doesn't it look awesome?

RUFUS. Yeah, it looks really good.

JAMIE. I seriously did most of it myself. New floors, new windows – like the whole deal. I was like down on my hands and knees, replacing all the baseboards and everything.

RUFUS. That's crazy.

JAMIE. I mean, I had an electrician come in and do some things I don't know how to do, and Baylor helped me out / a lot –

RUFUS. Baylor helped you?

JAMIE. Yeah, he was here almost as much / as me.

RUFUS. You let that guy handle power tools?

JAMIE. He actually really knows what he's doing.

RUFUS. Oh my god, that guy was such an idiot, though – didn't he like drive his car into the pond behind St. Michael's?

JAMIE. Yeah, in like tenth grade, / though.

RUFUS. *(Laughing.)* He got high on Robitussin? Or something and was like, "Jesus told me to drive my car into / the pond!"

JAMIE. Come on – he worked really hard on this, actually.

RUFUS. Well, don't be surprised if the walls start falling down around you.

JAMIE. People change, Rufus.

RUFUS. No no, they're just revealed over time.

JAMIE. What?

RUFUS. Nothing, I'm – Just something annoying I say to my students. I'm drunk.

> (**PETA** *appears from the house, wrapping a sweater or coat around herself.*)

Heyyy gal! Did we wake you up?

PETA. Why'd you let me pass out like that?!

RUFUS. You seemed exhausted, so –

PETA. What time did I fall asleep?

RUFUS. Like...nine?

PETA. Shit. Sorry guys.

RUFUS. You want a drink?

PETA. Uhhhh no, I'm okay.

RUFUS. Come onnn.

PETA. Nah, I'm good.

RUFUS. It's freezing out here!

PETA. True.

RUFUS. So have a drink to warm you up.

PETA. I'll just have a sip of yours.

RUFUS. Just have your own.

PETA. I only want a sip.

RUFUS. I'm just going to pour you a tiny glass.

PETA. I'm just going to have a sip of yours.

RUFUS. Okay.

PETA. Thank you.

       (She takes a small sip of his.)

RUFUS. Good, right?

PETA. Yeah.

RUFUS. You want your own?

PETA. Rufus.

JAMIE. Um – were you warm enough in there?

PETA. Yeah yeah, I was / fine.

RUFUS. Isn't she so pretty?

JAMIE. Yes.

PETA. All right, Rufus.

JAMIE. It can get pretty drafty up there, / so –

PETA. Oh, no, I was fine.

JAMIE. I'm gonna put in new windows in the upstairs soon. I reinstalled the downstairs ones this fall, but haven't gotten to the upstairs yet.

RUFUS. You. Are. So. Handy.

JAMIE. (*Shaking his head.*) You're trashed.

PETA. Yes, you have that look in your eye.

RUFUS. What look?

PETA. Unfocused. Like your eyes are looking at things but you're not really seeing what they are.

JAMIE. Yeah, totally!

PETA. See?

RUFUS. Shut up, both of you.

PETA. What've you boys been talking about?

RUFUS. GIRLS.

JAMIE. / Shut up.

PETA. Oooh, which girls?

RUFUS. Jamie's little co-worker.

PETA. She was very cute.

JAMIE. Okay, let's not –

PETA. Has anything ever happened between you?

RUFUS. You should at least make out with her in the back room or something – like all the flour and sugar raining down / around you –

PETA. Yes!

JAMIE. GUYS, guys, come on – no.

RUFUS. Okay, just / saying.

PETA. She's really cute!

JAMIE. I know. She is. It's just / not…

RUFUS. When was the last time you even dated anyone?! / And please don't say Melissa.

JAMIE. I don't know, not that long ago – No, it wasn't Melissa.

RUFUS. Mmmmkaaaayyyy.

JAMIE. Shut up.

OH – but wait, okay, so what we *should* talk about is that you sucker-punched a guy?!

PETA. Rufus! – Why do you have to tell that story / to EVERYONE –

RUFUS. Because it's an amazing story.

PETA. No, it's awful and embarrassing.

JAMIE. No it's not, it's awesome!

PETA. I shouldn't have done that.

JAMIE. YES you should / have.

RUFUS. It's one of the best things you've ever done!

PETA. He was a horrible idiot.

RUFUS. Yeah!

PETA. But I shouldn't have hit him.

RUFUS. He deserved it.

JAMIE. How did it feel – like, when you were hitting him?

PETA. Ohmygod, amazing. Amazing. Like – electric.

RUFUS. Yes!

PETA. And incredibly powerful.

JAMIE. Yeah.

PETA. *(Smiling.)* And he absolutely deserved it.

> *(She laughs.)*

God – yeah, it felt amazing!

RUFUS. Isn't she so fucking pretty?!

JAMIE. She is.

PETA. Rufus.

RUFUS. And she thinks her hair's falling out!

PETA. *(Smacking him.)* Rufus! Why would you say that?!

RUFUS. Sorry, but you're so pretty and it's ridiculous!

PETA. Don't just – say those things to people!

RUFUS. I'm a little drunk.

PETA. I see that.

RUFUS. Come ooonnn – have another sip.

PETA. No, thank you – I'm good.

> *(**RUFUS** nurses his drink, holding it between his palms and slowly, steadily sipping throughout the next section.)*

Jamie, this house is so cute.

JAMIE. Oh, thanks.

PETA. And the lake is beautiful.

JAMIE. Yeah, I like it.

PETA. It must be nice to get up every morning and look out at *this*.

JAMIE. It is, yeah.

PETA. *(Looking out.)* Yeah…it reminds me so much of this little place we used to go with my parents' friends, in Grasmere… It was / lovely in the same way.

RUFUS. Isn't she so cool?!

PETA. *(Shaking her head.)* Rufus.

JAMIE. Is your family still in England?

PETA. They are.

JAMIE. That's far away.

PETA. Yeah, yeah…it is. Though I'm a bit of a black sheep.

JAMIE. Why?

PETA. Ohhh I didn't go to Oxford, I didn't major in economics or business and I've invested in a career that they largely think is a waste of time, so.

RUFUS. And they just LOVE me.

PETA. They – Yeah. Well, to be fair, they only met you that once.

RUFUS. That seemed to be enough for them to form a pretty solid opinion.

PETA. They're – yeah. Very traditional.

JAMIE. Do you – were you supposed to have an arranged marriage or something?

RUFUS. Basically.

PETA. NO.

RUFUS. Please, they had a whole list of qualified suitors lined up for you.

JAMIE. Holy shit, / really?

PETA. No they did not. Not really.

JAMIE. Well do they know that Rufus is a genius?

RUFUS. Shut up.

JAMIE. / You are.

PETA. I've told them that, yes. Many times. They'll come around.

RUFUS. One day.

PETA. One day.

RUFUS. *(Banging down his empty glass and singing.)* ONNNNE DAAAAY. OKAY I HAVE TO TAKE A PISS.

> *(He stands unsteadily and begins to head toward the house.)*

JAMIE. Do you know where you're going?

RUFUS. *(Walking away.)* Shut up!

PETA. Do you need help in there?

RUFUS. Both of you, I am a fully-grown and capable PhD candidate, so shut the fuck up!

JAMIE. How did you get so drunk and I'm fine?!

RUFUS. I'm leaving you both behind!

> *(He disappears inside the house.)*

JAMIE. I'm sorry, I didn't realize how much he'd had.

PETA. That's okay. It's not your fault.

JAMIE. He used to hold his liquor better.

PETA. Well, he's getting older.

JAMIE. I guess so.

> *(A pause.)*

So Rufus says you work at a magazine?

PETA. Oh – yes. I'm an Associate Editor.

JAMIE. That's fancy.

PETA. Oh god, not really. I'm basically the editor's bitch.

JAMIE. Oh.

PETA. No, I'm kidding – I'm – I really love it, actually. And it's a beautiful magazine. We publish some really incredible writers and – yeah, I get to read all the new things that these amazing people are writing, / so –

JAMIE. Yeah, yeah. That's awesome.

You guys are like a power couple.

PETA. *(Laughing.)* Ha! – Right, yeah.

So...you've been renovating the house?

JAMIE. Yeah, for awhile now.

PETA. Your grandfather left it to you?

JAMIE. Yeah – to both of us, actually. But Rufus wasn't really into it.

PETA. I didn't know that.

JAMIE. Oh – yeah. This was a little while ago now, maybe before you guys / met...

PETA. It was sort of early on in our relationship when he died – I remember Rufus going to the funeral.

JAMIE. Okay, yeah, right... Aw – he should have brought you with him.

PETA. Oh, yeah, I – I guess I was working and it was such a short trip, I – / don't know.

JAMIE. Yeah, I guess he *was* only here for about six hours, so.

PETA. *(Looking at her hands.)* Right.

JAMIE. ...Yeah, but so I've been fixing it up since he died.

PETA. By yourself?

JAMIE. Pretty much, yeah.

PETA. That's impressive.

JAMIE. *(Shrugging.)* Aw – well – thanks – I mean, it's not done yet.

PETA. Yeah? What are your plans for it?

JAMIE. Uhhhh, well – geez, um – well, I want to replace the upstairs windows. And put in a skylight. And...I want to build another bedroom, or two actually, and then – well, actually, another little room that could be like a reading room? Something small but that gets a lot of light, with a couple of nice chairs and a rug and... maybe a piano? I don't play but feel like maybe my wife will? Or our kids will? I've always wanted one.

PETA. Wow. So, wife and kids, then.

JAMIE. Yeah. That's the dream, anyway.

PETA. How many?

JAMIE. Oh god – I don't know. Two? Three?

PETA. Yeah?

JAMIE. I mean, I'd totally adopt too, because I feel like there are so many kids who just get like tossed away, you know? Like I was watching this thing on TV and – they just kept saying how kids "slip through the cracks," and they kept showing this picture of this girl with these huge eyes and now it's like burned in my – Augh, anyway. But uhhh...yeah! Two or three?

PETA. *(Smiling.)* Yeah. Nice.

(She nods. They stare out at the water.)

How does he seem to you?

JAMIE. Rufus?

PETA. Yes.

JAMIE. Uhhhh fine? He's pretty drunk right now, / but...

PETA. Yeah.

JAMIE. Why?

PETA. Mmmm I don't know. I'm worried a little. I shouldn't have said anything.

JAMIE. Oh.

PETA. Never / mind.

JAMIE. Why are you worried?

PETA. Did he say anything to you?

JAMIE. He told me about his dissertation I guess.

PETA. *(Laughing.)* Oh really? He hardly says a thing about it to me. Every time I ask he's like, "Aughhhh I spent all day thinking about it, can we just talk about something else?!"

JAMIE. But, wait – why are you worried?

PETA. I – we are. I don't know. Experiencing. A thing.

JAMIE. Wow.

PETA. *(Laughing.)* Okay.

JAMIE. You guys are the shadiest.

PETA. I – don't want to say anything he / wouldn't want –

> (**RUFUS** *reappears.*)

RUFUS. Dude it's still pretty rustic in that bathroom! I think I got a splinter...

JAMIE. That's my next project.

RUFUS. *(Sitting down.)* What are you guys talking about?!

PETA. I've learned that Jamie's fixed this place up *by himself.*

RUFUS. He's the handiest.

PETA. Has your coworker seen this place?

JAMIE. Uhhh, no, not yet. I'll probably throw a party once it's finished.

PETA. Good, yes – she needs to see all the amazing craftsmanship / going on –

RUFUS. Yeah does she know that you're really handy? You have to tell her how incredibly handy you are.

JAMIE. / Stop saying handy.

PETA. *(Shaking her head.)* You're a mess.

RUFUS. *(Smirking.)* I know. But I'm gonna have just a liiiittle more.

> (*He pours more into his and* **JAMIE**'s *glasses, then dangles the bottle in front of* **PETA**'s *face.*)

Peeeta...you know you want some...

PETA. I'm good.

RUFUS. *(Dangling the bottle.)* Just a sip...?

PETA. I don't want any, Rufus.

RUFUS. *(Hypnotizing her with the bottle.)* I know somewhere in there is the party girl I know and love...

PETA. Yeah...I actually think I'm going back to bed. / Too cold out here for me.

RUFUS. No, come on! Stay up with us! You just have to drink more!

PETA. Nah...you guys have your brotherly time.

JAMIE. If you need another blanket I think there's one in that closet in your room.

PETA. Okay, thanks. Goodnight.

JAMIE. Goodnight.

PETA. Goodnight Rufus.

RUFUS. Isn't she so pretty?

JAMIE. Yes.

PETA. Goodnight Rufus.

JAMIE. / Goodnight.

RUFUS. No, staayyyy.

(*She leaves, disappearing into the house.*)

Augghhhh she's pissed.

JAMIE. Aw, she seems okay...

RUFUS. No she is, I see her little pissed-off face.

JAMIE. You want to go talk to her?

RUFUS. No, fuck it. I can't do it anymore.

JAMIE. You're...going through a thing?

RUFUS. Yeah, a thing. I guess it's a thing. I don't know. She thinks her hair's falling out all the time and I'm like, "It's just hormones, you'll be fine," but she's fixated on it, she's like counting the hairs in the shower drain. Ready?

(*He lifts his glass to toast.*)

JAMIE. Euughhh I don't know.

RUFUS. Come on come on. We have to finish it at this point.

JAMIE. Auuughhh I'm going to be worthless tomorrow. Okay, yes.

(*They clink glasses and drink.*)

The bathroom's not that bad.

RUFUS. I seriously got a splinter – look.

(*He holds out his hand.*)

JAMIE. From what?

RUFUS. The wall. I put my hand on the wall and got a splinter.

JAMIE. Well...sorry dude. It's my next project.

RUFUS. Imagining you and Baylor wielding power tools is amazing.

JAMIE. Why?

RUFUS. It just is. You have other plans for the place?

JAMIE. Yeah. I'm going to put an addition on the whole thing. I mean, I've got the land for it, / so...

RUFUS. ...Are you just pouring money into this thing?

JAMIE. No – I mean, not like th– not like you make it sound.

RUFUS. But how are you paying for it?

JAMIE. I have money saved. And Mom's helped me here and there.

RUFUS. You're using Mom's money on this?

JAMIE. Not like – Like she helped me with the electrician, stuff like that. What?

RUFUS. Nothing, I just...feel like she could be putting her money to better use.

JAMIE. *(Shaking his head.)* Okay well, when you're here driving her to the foot doctor and – whatever, checking her sugar levels, then you can tell her / that.

RUFUS. Jesus, okay – I'm just saying, / like –

JAMIE. What?

RUFUS. Don't – I don't know, just maybe don't put all your savings into this – / this –

JAMIE. Why?

RUFUS. It's just kind of sad.

> (**JAMIE** *shakes his head and stares down at the table.*)

Euuhhh, I'm – drunk and – saying stupid things I shouldn't.

JAMIE. Yeah.

RUFUS. YOU forced me to drink all this.

JAMIE. Okay.

RUFUS. And now all my terrible thoughts are spilling out.

JAMIE. Right.

...I'm going to head in, actually. I gotta work early, / so...

RUFUS. Yeah yeah, you should sleep.

JAMIE. You coming?

RUFUS. In a bit.

> (**JAMIE** *turns back to the house.*)

JAMIE. Well don't freeze to death.

RUFUS. Goodnight.

JAMIE. Night.

> (**JAMIE** *disappears inside the house.* **RUFUS**
> *looks out at the water, then rests his head on*
> *his arms.*)

3. The Bakery

(Late afternoon. **MARY** *reads a book at the bakery counter.)*

*(***DANNY*** *strides in, smirking.)*

DANNY. What up little sister.

MARY. *(Puzzled.)* Hey.

DANNY. Hey.

MARY. Did you walk here?

DANNY. No, hitched a ride from that Baylor kid.

MARY. I thought I was picking you up.

DANNY. Nah, you don't need to.

MARY. You're gonna walk out to the Walmart?

DANNY. Don't need to go to the Walmart.

MARY. Why?

DANNY. Because Ben Stirling called me.

MARY. No shit! Wait – the electrician guy?

DANNY. In Scranton, yeah. He wants me to come by his office, / so –

MARY. Today?

DANNY. Yes, today. Like, now.

MARY. That's awesome! Except… Shit – I can't leave right now, and Jamie's out on a / delivery –

DANNY. That's fine, I'm just gonna borrow your car.

MARY. Oh, really?

DANNY. Yes.

MARY. So how am I gonna get home?

DANNY. I'll come get you afterward. Or you COULD walk. It's not that far.

MARY. It's fucking freezing out.

DANNY. Then ask Jamie for a ride.

MARY. It's fine, I'll just walk.

DANNY. Come on, the guy called me and said *today*, I wasn't going to argue with / him –

MARY. No, I know – it's good, it's really good.

DANNY. I'm gonna get this job and get out of your hair.

MARY. You're not in my hair.

DANNY. Well, whatever – I'm in my own hair then.

    (A pause.)

MARY. So...what – he definitely wants to hire you?

DANNY. He said he wanted to talk about a job.

MARY. But is it full-time or contract / work...?

DANNY. He said he wanted to talk. That's all I know.

MARY. Okay, well – good.

DANNY. Yeah, it is good.

    (He shakes his head.)

You need to get laid my friend.

MARY. Shut up.

DANNY. You're allll wound up.

MARY. I am / not.

DANNY. You're all – like look at your shoulders, you're like walking around like –

    (He demonstrates walking around with his shoulders jacked up to his ears, goofy.)

MARY. *(Laughing.)* Shut up!

DANNY. You need to go out to Scranton and get freaky in a bar with some dude / or something.

MARY. Danny.

DANNY. Like in the bathroom stall.

MARY. Danny.

DANNY. Drink a few drinks, take off your hairnet...

MARY. *(Laughing.)* Shut up.

DANNY. Unless he's into that. Maybe he's into that. You still wearing those granny / panties?

MARY. Ohmygod leave me alone.

DANNY. Those big white things? 'Cause those'll go good with the / hairnet.

MARY. I haven't worn those since SIXTH GRADE.

DANNY. Really? Because I feel like I've seen your laundry lately...

MARY. Go away.

DANNY. And I feel like I saw a pair of biiiiig white granny panties hanging up / in the –

MARY. ONE PAIR, I have one pair I wear when I have to do my laundry and I have no other underwear left, okay, shut up!

DANNY. I thought so.

MARY. Go away.

DANNY. I'm going. Give me your keys, granny panty.

> *(She digs into her purse and throws the keys at him.)*

(Catching them with difficulty.) Jesus.

MARY. I hate you.

DANNY. I'll see you later.

> *(He turns to the door.)*

MARY. Break your legs.

DANNY. Hey – you want me to pick up a pizza or something on the way back?

MARY. Sure, yeah.

DANNY. ...You got some cash?

MARY. ...Yeah.

> *(She digs some cash out of her purse and tosses it to him.)*

DANNY. Thanks.

MARY. You're welcome. Hey – make sure you tell him about all that work you did for Dad on the house way back – that's relevant / experience.

DANNY. I know.

MARY. And that job you did in Nazareth – for that / contractor –

DANNY. GOODBYE.

(He waves over his shoulder as he starts out the door. **RUFUS** *walks in as* **DANNY** *is leaving.)*

DANNY. Holy shit.

RUFUS. Hey man!

DANNY. Holy fucking shit. Rufus Hewitt.

(He shakes **RUFUS**' *hand vigorously and pats him on the back.)*

Where the hell did you come from?

RUFUS. Uhhh, / I'm –

DANNY. How are you, man?

RUFUS. I'm good, I'm good. It's good to see you.

DANNY. Yeah! What – you should have told me you were in town, I would / have –

RUFUS. Yeah, it was kind of spur-of-the-moment, actually, we just decided to – I'm here with my girlfriend, so...

DANNY. Nice.

RUFUS. Yeah.

DANNY. Man. It's been a really long time.

RUFUS. Yeah I know.

DANNY. So, what – you been out curing cancer or...? We all figured you went off to like run NASA or something.

RUFUS. Nah... I've just been doing school, mostly. Getting my PhD.

DANNY. Well – That sounds about right.

RUFUS. Still a nerd.

DANNY. Yeah, no, that's good.

RUFUS. ...How about you?

DANNY. Well, I did two tours in / Afghanistan.

RUFUS. Oh right – wow. Yeah, Jamie / mentioned...

DANNY. 548th Combat Sustainment Support Battalion, 10th Sustainment Brigade, 10th Mountain Division.

RUFUS. Whoa.

DANNY. So. Yeah.

RUFUS. That must have been intense.

DANNY. ...Yeah. It was.

RUFUS. Yeah.

(*A pause.* **DANNY** *laughs a bit to himself.*)

DANNY. I actually thought about you.

RUFUS. Really?

DANNY. No – yeah, I did, because um – well, so there was this one night, pretty soon after I got there, and we were out on this night patrol?

RUFUS. ...Yeah.

DANNY. Yeah. So okay, so – we'd gotten a call from another platoon about this command wire leading into the ground, right? So then we have to – we go out there to escort the EOD team, right, and we're like squeezing down these narrow alleyways and shitty roads, and like...and I mean literal shit – like the whole place reeked of shit – but, so... Okay, so we just gotta get like a mile and a half through the center of this village to where the other platoon's guarding the IED...but then we get there and it's just barely after midnight and fucking FREEZING, like negative twenty and all the dogs in the village are howling their faces off and we get there but then we gotta wait till the top of the next hour to blow the thing, right?

RUFUS. Oh... / yeah?

DANNY. Because we can only do controlled detonations at the top of the hour – which is some kind of an attempt at don't-kill-civilians-thing – but we missed top of the hour by like three minutes – so then we all have to just – well, we're all just standing there and staring out at this thing, like staring at this stupid wire, all of us, just these rows of guys staring – WAITING – in the freezing fucking cold – and after like twenty minutes, this kid next to me, Rodriguez, starts *singing* really, really quiet.

(*He pauses and smiles at* **RUFUS**, *looking for a reaction.*)

RUFUS. ...Yeah?

DANNY. Yeah, so he's this kid from Ohio, nice kid – and like he has this face that always makes him look surprised or...in *awe* of shit or something...but, so... Okay, so I leaned over a little, because I thought I heard something, but I wasn't sure, like I didn't believe that this little dude would be making any sound at all, so I lean over and for real – like for real for real – really quiet he's singing YOUR SONG.

RUFUS. *(Confused.)* ...Oh...

DANNY. You know, come on.

RUFUS. Shit, / ummmm.

DANNY. No, come ON.

RUFUS. IIII'm an asshole, I –?

DANNY. Seriously?

RUFUS. Shit, I don't know...

DANNY. You seriously don't remember?!

RUFUS. I'm – old and can't / remember anything...

MARY. Danny, you should seriously go if you're gonna make / it on time.

> (**DANNY** *sings a few lines from "The Weight"*
> *by The Band.*[*] **RUFUS** *smiles nervously.*
> **DANNY** *continues singing. Eventually,* **RUFUS**
> *joins in on the last few lines of the chorus.)*

RUFUS. Jesus, yeah...

DANNY. You used to play that shit in your car like every day.

RUFUS. Yeah, I guess / I did.

---

[*]A license to produce *Five Mile Lake* does not include a performance license for "The Weight." The publisher and author suggest that the licensee contact ASCAP or BMI to ascertain the music publisher and contact such music publisher to license or acquire permission for performance of the song. If a license or permission is unattainable for "The Weight," the licensee may not use the song in *Five Mile Lake* but may create an original composition in a similar style or use a similar song in the public domain. For further information, please see Music Use Note on page 3.

DANNY. When we'd be driving around wherever, like on all the back roads to Scranton and you'd be *blasting* that shit.

RUFUS. God, yeah. I was such a / dork.

DANNY. No, but I loved it. And that's a great fucking song.

RUFUS. Yeah, no, it is for sure. / "The Weight."

DANNY. I swear we had that song on loop – right – like it'd end and then we'd just / play it again –

MARY. Danny, you should / get going.

RUFUS. Right – yes – we used to scream it out the windows.

DANNY. YES!

RUFUS. Like in the parking lot at the diner / – trying to like –

DANNY. Ohmygod, yes dude.

RUFUS. Trying to freak out all the old ladies.

DANNY. I loved that shit! Auuughhh!

MARY. Danny.

DANNY. *(To* **MARY.***)* I know!

Augh. Anyway, man. I thought about you. While I was freezing my balls off.

RUFUS. Well – thanks, that's –

DANNY. And then we all started in with Rodriguez...just reeeally quiet, like way under our breath, trying to forget that we were freezing our asses off.

RUFUS. Yeah.

DANNY. *(His face growing dark.)* He was a funny kid.

> *(He stares into space for a moment;* **MARY** *tenses and starts to approach. He shakes it off.)*

Um. When're you leaving?

RUFUS. Uh, not sure yet. Peta has to get back for work, so...

DANNY. Pe-ta?

RUFUS. My girlfriend.

DANNY. Where's she from?

RUFUS. Uhhhh, mostly raised in London...

DANNY. Whoa, / nice.

RUFUS. But she lived all over Southern Asia and in Dubai, actually, / as a kid.

DANNY. Yikes dude. You don't mess / around!

MARY. DANNY, seriously –

DANNY. *(Snapping.) What?!* Can't I just talk to someone for a fucking minute?

> (**MARY** *shrinks back.* **RUFUS** *glances at her.* **DANNY** *turns back to* **RUFUS**.)

Sorry, just – Um. So – hey – let's grab a beer before you go.

RUFUS. Definitely.

DANNY. We can drive out to Scranton or something. Go to the diner.

RUFUS. Ha – Perfect. I'll look for my old mixtapes.

DANNY. Nice. Well – I gotta go. Gotta go see about a job!

RUFUS. Oh – / nice.

DANNY. But, really good to see you, man.

RUFUS. Yeah, you too.

DANNY. Thanks for the car, little sister.

MARY. Yup.

> *(She waves half-heartedly as he leaves.)*

Good luck!

> (**DANNY** *is gone. A pause. She looks at the floor, exhales, then up at* **RUFUS**.)

Sorry about / that.

RUFUS. Oh my god, no – Don't be sorry.

MARY. He gets a little...

RUFUS. No, it's fine – it's good to see him.

MARY. Okay...good. I know he was glad to see you.

RUFUS. I feel bad I didn't – I hope I didn't get him / worked up or...

MARY. No no, that's just – He gets kind of hyper sometimes.

RUFUS. Yeah. Right.

> (*He looks out to the parking lot, after* **DANNY**, *thoughtful.*)

MARY. Um, can I get you anything?

RUFUS. *(Turning back.)* Oh – I'm okay.

MARY. You're looking for Jamie?

RUFUS. I was, yeah.

MARY. He went out on a delivery – but he'll probably go straight home after – I think he said that was his plan.

RUFUS. Oh, okay. Hmmm. Well.

MARY. You can call him, though, I'm sure he has his phone.

RUFUS. Yeahhhh, that's okay. Shit.

MARY. ...What?

RUFUS. I actually came to – well I just said some things last night and – I was coming to apologize to him.

MARY. What'd you say?

RUFUS. Not totally sure...but I think his feelings were hurt.

MARY. He seemed fine.

RUFUS. Well he was likely just hiding his pain from you.

MARY. Maybe.

RUFUS. He definitely was.

MARY. Okay.

RUFUS. Inside he is crying and terribly upset.

MARY. I didn't know that.

RUFUS. Yeah, I may have shattered his utopian vision for himself.

MARY. What did you say?

RUFUS. Uhhhh I don't know – I was just an asshole to him about his whole fixing up the lake house thing.

MARY. Ahhh.

RUFUS. I basically told him it was a waste of time and money / so –

MARY. Eeee – that's like his baby.

RUFUS. I know.

MARY. He's definitely crying inside.

RUFUS. I know. He made me drink all this whiskey and....
Ugh. Anyway. Um – thanks. I'll look for him back at
the house.

MARY. Okay.

(He turns back to the door.)

Actually – do you want to take some of these?

(She points to the leftover muffins.)

I gotta close soon. And they're still good. You could pop
them in the toaster oven and you guys could have them
for breakfast or something tomorrow.

RUFUS. Whoa. Yeah, actually. I will totally do that.

(He comes back over to the counter to browse.)

Oh man, YES, I love these things. With the streusel
stuff on top?

MARY. Me too. I had to make a serious limit for myself or I
would just eat a million a day.

RUFUS. Yeah. Actually... Do you care if I have one now? I
just realized that I'm starving and horribly hungover.

MARY. Oh – yeah, totally. Here –

(She grabs a little plate for him.)

RUFUS. Thanks.

*(He eats. She packs up leftover muffins,
including a separate bag for* **RUFUS.***)*

MARY. Does your girlfriend – would she want something?
We also have all these / cookies –

RUFUS. Oh, no, she has this thing against sugar these days.

MARY. Oh. Well that's probably good.

RUFUS. Really?

MARY. Yeah, isn't sugar proven to be the worst thing you
could possibly ever eat or something?

RUFUS. It's that bad?

MARY. I think it like, melts your organs and makes you fatter than fat does.

RUFUS. Well, shit. I'm screwed.

MARY. Me too. I'm addicted to gummy worms.

RUFUS. Seriously?

MARY. YES.

RUFUS. Then your organs are completely melted.

MARY. Probably, yes.

RUFUS. Nah – you're all runner healthy, you'll be fine.

MARY. What?

RUFUS. Aren't you a runner?

MARY. Uhhh – yeah, I was – I mean, I / am...

RUFUS. Yeah, I used to drive past you out on Brakefield Road in the middle of the night.

MARY. You did?

RUFUS. Yeah, weren't you always out there, like racing through the shadows?

MARY. You would drive past / me?

RUFUS. Yeah. And you were very... I don't know – you know when you can look at someone and know that they're really good at what they're doing, like there's this kind of grace to them as they're doing the thing that they're doing and you can see, like, oh yeah, that girl's really good.

MARY. Ummmm thank you.

RUFUS. So you still do it?

MARY. Uhhh, sometimes, yeah. It's hard to find time for it.

RUFUS. How far do you go?

MARY. Usually just like five miles.

RUFUS. Whoa – that's hardcore.

MARY. Not really – I used to go, like nine or ten. But now I've kind of plateaued at five.

RUFUS. Still, that's way better than I could do.

(He finishes the muffin.)

RUFUS. Well. That was awesome.

MARY. Good.

RUFUS. I should get going probably.

MARY. Okay.

> *(She hands him a bakery bag.)*

Here you are.

RUFUS. Thank you. I'm going to get really fat.

MARY. Yes.

RUFUS. Don't agree with me!

MARY. Well, share them with your girlfriend.

RUFUS. Yeah, I'll force some cookies down her throat.

MARY. While she's sleeping.

RUFUS. *(Wiggling his fingers evilly.)* Yessss, she'll never know.

> **(MARY** *laughs. He looks at the bag and sighs.)*

MARY. Well. If Jamie stops here first for some reason, I'll tell him you're looking for him.

RUFUS. Thanks. Yeah.

> *(He stands still and doesn't leave. She peers at him, amused.)*

Can I admit something to you, Mary?

MARY. Sure…

RUFUS. Since you've already watched me stuff a giant muffin in my face and I can't hide anything from you now?

MARY. Yeah.

RUFUS. …I really don't want to go back there.

MARY. Why?

RUFUS. *(Laughing.)* Aughhhh what's wrong with me, I suck so much. I just…don't want to face anything? I guess? Whenever I come back here I'm like, "How the hell did I live here for EIGHTEEN YEARS?"

MARY. …So why're you here?

RUFUS. Well, Jamie's here.

MARY. *(Peering at him.)* Yeah...

RUFUS. You're looking at me with a face.

MARY. I – sorry.

RUFUS. No – what?

MARY. Well, you're not here to see Jamie.

RUFUS. *(Laughing.)* Geez! Okay... Well, Mary. You're very astute.

MARY. You guys aren't very close.

RUFUS. Not terribly, no.

MARY. I mean, you're just very different.

RUFUS. Yup – He plays paintball for fun! Um – Do you mind if I just hide out here for a little bit?

MARY. No, go for it.

RUFUS. Thank you.

MARY. Eat some muffins.

RUFUS. Hey – yeah. I will.

> *(He opens the bag and starts eating another muffin.)*

MARY. So if you're not here to see Jamie...

RUFUS. I think I'm supposed to be working on my relationship.

MARY. That doesn't sound good.

RUFUS. Nope.

MARY. Do you want some gummy worms?

> *(He looks up at her and laughs.)*

RUFUS. You just happen to have some?

MARY. I told you I have a problem.

RUFUS. Ummm yes. I would love some gummy worms.

MARY. Okay, one sec.

> *(She disappears in the back and returns with a huge bag of gummy worms.)*

RUFUS. It's fucking huge!

MARY. I know – I buy them at Costco.

RUFUS. Jesus.

MARY. Don't judge me.

RUFUS. I'm not, I'm thrilled – about how many gummy worms you have.

MARY. Help yourself.

> *(She hands him the bag.)*

RUFUS. Thank you.

> *(They both eat gummy worms, chewing in quiet for a moment.)*

These are really fucking good.

MARY. I know.

> *(They chew.)*

I'm serious, when your day is shit, just get yourself a bag of these.

RUFUS. I will. Do you do the sour ones too?

MARY. No, just classic.

RUFUS. I always kind of liked the sour / ones.

MARY. But you can't get those in an enormous bag.

RUFUS. Oh no?

MARY. Nope, so stick to the old school gummy, I say.

RUFUS. Yeah.

> *(He smiles at her.)*

MARY. What?

RUFUS. So what are you doing here?

MARY. Uhhh...

RUFUS. I mean...what are you *still* doing here?

MARY. Ah.

RUFUS. Because...and forgive me if this is totally presumptuous, but I think you're very much like me.

MARY. Yeah...

RUFUS. You think the lake is horribly depressing and the people are horribly ignorant and the whole town feels like...

MARY. Small and grey and awful. Yeah.

RUFUS. So...you're sticking around for Danny?

MARY. (*Shrugging.*) I... – Yes, I guess. I mean... I had a job at Lehigh, after I graduated from there, and I was dating Jared... Do you remember Jared Kane? – Yeah, so, I was with him and I was thinking, cool, yeah, I'll take a couple years and save up and apply for my masters and we'll move far away and all will be well... but then our dad got sick, so I came home to help him, and then...my relationship bombed and our dad died and Danny came back... That "couple years" of treading water turned into like...eight.

RUFUS. Right. I'm sorry about your dad.

MARY. Oh – thanks.

So, anyway...

RUFUS. It's not too late, you know.

MARY. Ehh...

RUFUS. It's totally not. You could get up and get in your car and leave tomorrow.

MARY. Right.

RUFUS. I'm serious. People do it. All the time. I did it.

MARY. I can't just...disappear like that.

RUFUS. I bet you Danny would understand.

MARY. Yeah, I don't know... He's really broke.

RUFUS. But he's also an adult with a lot of experience who can figure something out.

MARY. He actually might be getting a job today.

RUFUS. Right – see? So go – do your life. Your masters?

MARY. Yeah.

RUFUS. For?

MARY. French?

RUFUS. French!

MARY. Yeah I know, it's completely worthless in the real world, / but...

RUFUS. No, no –

MARY. I was a French major. And I wanted to run away and be in Paris and just – God, I don't know, smoke cigarettes and wander the streets late at night and sleep with painters and be a different person with a life.

RUFUS. *(Smiling.)* ...Right.

MARY. So.

RUFUS. Well... I don't know if you want to be in New York at all...but there's always a lot of jobs at the university. I mean, that could be good while you look for something you really want or apply for school or whatever – I can totally put in a good word for you, just let me / know.

MARY. Really?

RUFUS. Absolutely. But you gotta get yourself there first.

MARY. *(Laughing.)* Okay, yeah...

> *(She laughs sadly to herself; then something very small and solemn passes over her face. He sees it.)*
>
> *(Shaking it off, laughing.)*

Euughhhh I feel like I'm drowning here sometimes.

RUFUS. *(Quiet.)* Yeah. You're like me.

Well I might get kicked out of my PhD program. If it makes you / feel better.

MARY. Why?

RUFUS. I haven't met any of my deadlines. In...like...a year.

MARY. Oh no.

RUFUS. I'm supposed to be writing this – my dissertation. And. I can't do it.

MARY. Have you written any of it?

RUFUS. Ehhhh I just – basically write the same paragraph over and over again, like I'm the guy in *The Shining* – like I'm writing in circles, and – lately it's gotten so bad, I – / I'm just completely...

MARY. What?

RUFUS. Ohhh, I just go to my little carrel in the library and I write little notes on little notecards and open and close books and map out useless outlines – and then I go to the movies!

MARY. And see what?

RUFUS. Oh, the most dreadful things I can possibly see. Things with – Adam Sandler* or something.

MARY. Oh *no*.

RUFUS. And then I go home with all my books and my half-assed outlines and all my little notes about nothing, and I'm like, "Oh man I'm so brain-dead from all the work I've been doing!" Which is a just a total lie, so – Yeah. That drowning thing. Me too.

(*A pause.*)

MARY. What's it about?

RUFUS. Uhhhh it's *supposed* to be about the laments for the dead in Greek tragedy...and in *Homer*, but...

MARY. Wow.

RUFUS. But right now it's about fuck-all.

MARY. Is Antigone in it?

RUFUS. (*Laughing.*) She is! – I mean, she's supposed / to be.

MARY. I loved that play.

RUFUS. Yeah?

MARY. There was this famous company, I guess, that did it in New York, and Mrs. Torrance took our whole AP class to see it. I still remember it so vividly – they had these beautiful masks they all wore... It was just – well, I thought it was amazing.

RUFUS. Yeah, it's a good one. God. Mrs. Torrance. I forgot about her...

MARY. Yeah, she was awesome. With those / glasses –

RUFUS. God, her glasses! Yes.

(*He laughs and rubs his eyes, then stares at the gummy worms in his hand. She watches him.*)

*Author's Note: When this name is no longer relevant, it can be replaced with the name of another similar celebrity who has made a similar series of terrible movies.

MARY. I knew it was you.

RUFUS. What?

MARY. When I'd be out running, I knew it was you when you drove past.

RUFUS. Really?

MARY. I'd see your car coming...and then I'd start running really fast and I'd put on this face, like, I don't know... like try to look very serene and steady or something.

RUFUS. You never waved at me.

MARY. I know, I was trying to look serene and focused! And you were Danny's friend, so... I don't know.

RUFUS. What.

MARY. I was shy. And I liked you.

RUFUS. You did?

MARY. You knew I did, don't pretend.

RUFUS. Okay, I knew.

MARY. Yeah, so –

RUFUS. Whenever I came over, you always managed to be sunbathing.

MARY. Shut up!

RUFUS. Even in like, / October.

MARY. Oh god shut / up.

RUFUS. And I was like, "Danny, isn't your sister cold / out there?"

MARY. I hate you.

RUFUS. And he was like, "Dude, stop looking at my sister!"

(They laugh. MARY's eyes get sad.)

(Standing.) Well...I should...

MARY. *(Standing.)* Yeah.

RUFUS. Ohhhh what are we gonna do, Mary?

MARY. I don't know.

RUFUS. Run off into the night I guess.

MARY. I guess so.

RUFUS. Just be mystical nighttime creatures and forget about everything else.

MARY. *(Smiling.)* That sounds…amazing.

RUFUS. Yeah.

(He turns toward the door, car keys in hand.)

Well –

MARY. Actually – would you mind giving me a ride home? Danny took my car and / it's freezing out –

RUFUS. Oh my god – of course.

MARY. Yeah?

RUFUS. Yes. It would be my pleasure.

MARY. Okay. Thank you.

4. The Backyard

(*Evening. The sound of water knocking against the dock.* **PETA** *sits in a decrepit lawn chair in the backyard, tucked into herself, reading, her phone nearby.*)

(**JAMIE** *approaches from the house.*)

JAMIE. Hey.

PETA. *(Turning.)* Oh – hey. Where's Rufus?

JAMIE. Uhhhh I don't know. He's not here?

PETA. I thought he was with you.

JAMIE. With me? No...

PETA. He said he was going to find you. He didn't call you?

JAMIE. No. Why was he looking for me?

PETA. He said he felt bad about – something from last night.

JAMIE. Oh reeeally? / Okay.

PETA. He said he was going to stop in at the bakery –

JAMIE. Oh, shit – yeah, I was out on a delivery, so maybe I missed / him.

PETA. But that was hours ago now.

JAMIE. Did you call him?

PETA. Yup.

JAMIE. Hmm...well, he may not get good service around here – it can be kind of spotty.

PETA. Mmm... I think he's just being willfully ignorant of my phone calls.

JAMIE. Ah.

PETA. He can be a real piece of shit like that.

JAMIE. Yeah, I – yeah.

...Was he hungover this morning?

PETA. Well he slept until two, so...

JAMIE. Eeee.

PETA. Lots of great quality time for us!

JAMIE. Right. Were you up early?

PETA. Yeah, I can't sleep past seven. So I walked around the lake some. And I've been reading... Might as well get some work done, right?

(She grimaces and tosses her work onto her bag.)

JAMIE. He's probably just driving around. He used to like to do that – just drive around aimlessly.

PETA. Yes, he seems to want to be lost, so –

(She shakes her head, looking out at the water. **JAMIE** *eyes her, then turns back to the house.)*

JAMIE. Well, are you hungry? I could make us some / food –

PETA. I mean, am I crazy?

JAMIE. ...I don't –

PETA. Is he just a horrible dick and I've just been pretending this whole time that that's okay?

JAMIE. Uh, well –

PETA. I mean, he's the world's most spectacular narcissist, right?!

JAMIE. Uhh.

PETA. And I think I've been going along believing that it's all right and it's surmountable and that we'll be fine because we're meant for each other or some shit, but now, I don't know, I'm worried that ultimately, at his core, he's – just a really, deeply selfish person.

JAMIE. Uhhhh... He can be pretty selfish, yeah.

PETA. Right?!

JAMIE. Yes.

PETA. Okay – Thank you!

JAMIE. I mean...he...basically hasn't like, talked to me, really, in like...since he came for Paw Paw's funeral. Like I've called him – and he doesn't call back – and then like a week later I'll get an email that's like, oh sorry I missed your call, I'm just really busy and blah blah.

PETA. Right.

JAMIE. Which is clearly just a – he's not sorry, he's just trying to relieve his guilt. And I'm like, okay, cool, yeah, I get it, but like, just – can you call Mom like maybe once a week or – something – so that I don't have to do EVERYTHING – you know? – Sorry.

PETA. No.

JAMIE. It's a lot.

PETA. It totally is.

JAMIE. PLUS, like – dude, just stay for your fucking grandfather's funeral, you know?!

PETA. Wait – He didn't stay for the whole thing?

JAMIE. No, I mean, he did, technically – but he left right afterward. Like we had a reception thing after and he was there for about ten minutes and then was just like, I gotta get back, so – he disappeared.

PETA. God, yeah, he – barely said anything about it, I remember he was just like – hey, gotta go to this funeral...

JAMIE. Yeah, / well.

PETA. He made it seem like he barely knew the man.

JAMIE. I mean, maybe they weren't close, but – still – like, he should be there for *me* and Mom – he should BE there –

PETA. Yeah.

JAMIE. Eugh – anyway, whatever, / sorry...

PETA. No no no – You're right.

(*She shakes her head and closes her eyes for a moment, laughing to herself.*)

Gaaaahhhh everything's a mess.

JAMIE. ...What's going on with you guys?

PETA. Uhhhh, well...we lost a baby.

JAMIE. Oh / no.

PETA. I was thirteen weeks. Just when you think you're safe! ...

JAMIE. Shit. I'm – god. I'm sorry – Rufus didn't say a / thing –

PETA. No, he's been pretty quiet about it. So then I've been... We've both just been very quiet.

JAMIE. Did you guys plan... / or –

PETA. No, no. No, it was all a surprise. And at first, you know, I really didn't want it, actually... Like I thought, oh NO no no...and then – I did. And...I had really imagined him, you know?

JAMIE. Yeah.

PETA. Like I really saw this whole – life.

> *(She laughs and shakes her hands in the air, trying to explain.)*

I shouldn't have done that I guess!

> *(She puts her hand on her chest.)*

I need to – Uh. I don't know, um –?

JAMIE. Why don't you come inside?

PETA. You know like when your heart is like – *(She gestures.)* pounding so fast you can like *eugh* – and / it's like –

JAMIE. I guess / I...

PETA. Like relentless and awful – Could you...get me some water, actually?

JAMIE. Sure – yeah, of / course.

PETA. Thank you.

JAMIE. You okay?

PETA. Yeah.

> *(She takes a breath.)*

Yeah, thanks.

JAMIE. Okay, I'll be right back.

PETA. Thank you.

> *(She nods and he turns back to the house, then disappears inside.)*
>
> *(She stares out for a long moment, breathing. Then unzips her boots and strips off her coat. She strides toward the water, breathing, and disappears.)*

5. The Bathtub

> (**PETA** *in the bathtub, shivering.* **JAMIE** *sits on the toilet, his eyes closed, breathing hard; his leg is shaking.*)

JAMIE. Warming up?

PETA. Yeah.

JAMIE. You sure?

PETA. Yeah.

JAMIE. You sure?

PETA. Yeah.

> (*He shakes his head emphatically.*)

JAMIE. You scared the shit out of me.

PETA. I'm sorry.

JAMIE. You could have had a heart attack.

PETA. No, / I –

JAMIE. You could have had a heart attack and died and then I'd have to explain to Rufus that I let his girlfriend / throw herself into –

PETA. You're not responsible.

JAMIE. If you jump into a half-frozen lake at MY house while I'M the only one around, then yeah, YES, I am completely responsible for you.

PETA. I'm sorry.

JAMIE. Yeah.

PETA. You're right. It wasn't fair to you.

JAMIE. No.

PETA. I wasn't thinking about that.

> (*He opens his eyes. He looks at the floor, his leg still shaking.*)

I really am sorry.

JAMIE. (*Quiet.*) Were you trying to?

PETA. What.

JAMIE. To – kill yourself?

PETA. No.

JAMIE. Okay.

I'm just wondering if – I mean, there's…hotlines and things we can call – or just – we can go to the hospital if you / want –

PETA. I wasn't trying to kill myself.

JAMIE. Okay.

PETA. I was trying to…break through something?

JAMIE. Okay…

PETA. I just thought – if I can – I don't know, if I can just push through and get to the other side of this whole thing, then, yeah, something – will be better. Or clearer. I know I seem crazy to you.

JAMIE. No – just –

PETA. What?

JAMIE. I don't totally understand it.

PETA. …I know.

> *(She nods. Then she tucks her knees to her chest and rocks a bit.)*

I was thinking about – This is weird – but this thing kind of popped into my head, like it came out of the cold, this – Nathaniel Hawthorne quote I used to love? It's like, um – "No one will flourish any more than a potato, if planted and replanted too many times in the same worn-out soil. My children have had other birthplaces, and as long as their fortunes are in my control, they will strike their roots into unaccustomed earth."

JAMIE. Huh.

PETA. I loved that…because I'm doing this totally different thing from my parents and I'm being this person they never imagined I'd be and that's been – hard – I mean, I really had to make my own way, you know? And I'm proud of that, I'm really proud, actually…but, at the same time…I've pushed myself so far away from them in every way and... I don't know, all of a sudden I miss being part of a whole, you know, rather than just this – weird root struck down in its own soil... I mean, I look at you and I think, yes, you've done it right, you can just drive over to your mother's house and help her when she's sick and you're building a whole amazing *place* for yourself, and / I'm –

JAMIE. Yeah, but I'm just – I mean you guys are doing the big things.

PETA. I don't know if that's true.

JAMIE. *(Shrugging.)* Eh. Well – Does your family know about the – that you...

PETA. No.

JAMIE. Maybe you should call them.

PETA. *(Smiling.)* ...See, when you say it, it sounds so simple.

    (The sound of **RUFUS** *entering the house.* **JAMIE** *stiffens and stands.)*

RUFUS. *(From offstage.)* Hello?

PETA. *(Yelling.)* RUFUS?

JAMIE. *(Standing.)* I'm going / to –

RUFUS. *(Appearing in the doorway.)* Hey –

    (Seeing **JAMIE.***)*

Whoa what the hell is this?

PETA. Where were you?

RUFUS. What is going on?

JAMIE. She jumped in the lake.

RUFUS. WHAT?

JAMIE. And I had to get her body temperature back up quickly, / so –

RUFUS. *(To* **PETA.***)* Are you serious – What are you doing?

PETA. Swimming.

RUFUS. Peta – you seriously could've killed / yourself –

JAMIE. She's okay.

RUFUS. It's like subzero temperatures out there, you can't just jump into / the water –

PETA. *(Standing up.)* I JUMPED IN THE LAKE. And the world didn't implode on itself, and nobody died, so let's talk about something else, like where the fuck were you?

> *(She stands there, dripping. They are all quiet for a moment.* JAMIE *looks to the ground.)*

RUFUS. I – went to the bakery looking for Jamie and I ran into Mary and she needed a ride home.

JAMIE. Mary did?

RUFUS. So I drove her home.

PETA. For six hours?

JAMIE. What happened to her car?

RUFUS. Danny took it. No, I – we – drove around for awhile.

JAMIE. With Mary.

RUFUS. *Yes* – she was...freaking out about Danny and I felt like I had to – / I don't know –

PETA. You're a piece of shit.

RUFUS. Peta, come on.

JAMIE. What happened with Danny?

RUFUS. Nothing – Dude, can you give us some / privacy?

JAMIE. But why was she upset?

RUFUS. Because, I don't know! – She's trapped here wasting her life? Because everything about this place depresses the shit out of her?! – I don't know, Jamie. Can you please *please* leave us alone?

> *(He gestures toward the door.* JAMIE *shakes his head.)*

JAMIE. *(Quiet.)* You're a dick, Rufus.

RUFUS. Jamie, I'm not a dick because I let a girl who was visibly upset talk to me.

JAMIE. Okay, well your girlfriend just tried to drown herself, so maybe you should spend more time talking / to her.

PETA. Jamie.

JAMIE. I mean, you have officially become a negligent dick, so – good / job!

RUFUS. Yes, and good job on you – you've managed to remain an amazingly useless doormat.

> *(JAMIE shakes his head, looking at the floor. He glances up at PETA.)*

JAMIE. *(To PETA.)* I'll leave you alone.

> *(He exits quickly. RUFUS and PETA stare at each other. RUFUS closes the door. PETA hugs herself in the water. He sits on the toilet and rubs his hands over his face several times. A long moment. He looks at her.)*

RUFUS. Don't – jump into frozen lakes, Peta.

PETA. Don't disappear for hours and hours and not answer my phone calls.

RUFUS. So this was some kind of act of revenge?

PETA. No.

RUFUS. Really.

PETA. Really.

What is going on with you?

> *(He shakes his head, looking down.)*

You'd rather drive around with a random girl from town than talk to me?

RUFUS. No.

PETA. That's how it feels.

RUFUS. No – I'm – I don't know...

PETA. You're what, Rufus? You're angry? You're sad? You want out of this whole / thing?

RUFUS. No – that's –

> *(He takes in a long breath. He looks at her.)*

I – can't write anything. At all. And it's...really bad. Like, I've never... It's really bad.

PETA. ...Wait, so...

RUFUS. Like I'm completely paralyzed.

I haven't written anything Real in over a year.

PETA. Rufus.

RUFUS. So.

PETA. What have you been doing all day?

RUFUS. Nothing. I just sit in the library and then I go to the movies.

PETA. For a year?

> *(He nods his head, looking down. **PETA** shivers. She gets out of the bath and grabs a towel from the rack, stares at her hand, then wraps the towel around herself. She sits on the edge of the tub and looks at her hands.)*

I think I just got a splinter.

RUFUS. Let me see.

> *(She shows him her hand. He takes it.)*

PETA. See it?

RUFUS. Yeah.

> *(He works on extracting the splinter.)*

I wanted to tell you but – I didn't know how.

PETA. Why?

RUFUS. Because...I'm embarrassed. Because you are someone who is successful in every single thing you do, who has never failed at anything, who is practical to your core, and it's embarrassing – I mean what are you going to say when I turn to you in the middle of the night and say, hey, I'm lost and flailing around in my life?

PETA. That you'll get through it. And I know what failure feels like – What do you think I've felt like for the past few months?

RUFUS. ...I know.

> *(He nods. She squints. He pulls out her splinter and holds it up.)*

Got it.

PETA. I'm really really sad, Rufus.

RUFUS. I know. Me too.

PETA. I started thinking maybe you were relieved.

RUFUS. No. No. I mean... I was completely completely shit-storm terrified by it, but, I wanted – I mean, it was going to be ours. I wanted that.

PETA. Yeah. Me too.

> (*They are quiet for a moment.*)

RUFUS. (*Shaking his head, a small laugh.*) ...Euughh really great trip, huh?

PETA. (*Laughing too, sadly.*) Yeahhhh.
  I don't know what to do now.

> (*She looks at the wall; he looks at her.*)

6. The Bakery

> *(Early morning – very, very cold.* **JAMIE**
> *prepares to open, brewing coffee, arranging
> the case, going through the ritual of opening
> the bakery, only by himself. After a bit, he
> stands still and stares at the coffee, his mind
> elsewhere. Eventually he shakes his head
> and jumps up on the counter to write on
> the chalkboard.* **MARY** *unlocks the door and
> comes in, rushed, very bundled up. She's
> wearing lipstick.)*

MARY. Hey.

JAMIE. *(Looking over his shoulder.)* Hey.

MARY. *(Taking off her coat, etc.)* Sorry.

JAMIE. S'okay.

MARY. *(Heading into the back to hang up her coat.)* I totally
overslept. I don't know why my alarm didn't go off, but
– / it didn't, so –

JAMIE. You're fine, we still have time.

> *(She disappears in the back.* **JAMIE** *pauses,
> then continues writing on the chalkboard.)*
>
> *(She re-emerges, wearing her apron and
> tying her hair into a bun. She busies herself
> rearranging the case. There is a tiny, tiny
> smile on her face, some kind of levity that
> hasn't been there before.)*
>
> *(***JAMIE** *jumps down from the counter. He
> drums his fingers on the counter, pretending
> to be contemplating something work-related.*
> **MARY** *switches the placement of a couple of
> the trays in the case.)*

You don't like how I did it?

MARY. What? Oh, no – I just – usually do it, so –

JAMIE. So you don't like the way I did it.

MARY. No, I just – blueberry goes here and I always put the pumpkin below, so.

JAMIE. Okay.

MARY. I'm kind of OCD about it, / don't take it personally.

JAMIE. You think?

MARY. Do you really care?

JAMIE. No, I'm just – messing with you.
Ready?

MARY. Yup.

> *(He goes and unlocks the door, then walks back behind the counter. They are quiet again.)*

JAMIE. Big crowd.

MARY. Yup.

JAMIE. I guess it's really cold today.

MARY. Yeah it's fucking awful.

JAMIE. I think it was like, nine degrees when I left my house.

MARY. Yeah, it was about that at mine too.

JAMIE. Did you, uhh…watch the hockey game?

MARY. You know the answer to that.

JAMIE. It was a reeeeally good game.

MARY. I'm sure it was.

JAMIE. Team USA killed Slovakia.

MARY. Great.

JAMIE. Like KILLED them.

MARY. Amazing.

JAMIE. Like they were crying.

MARY. I'm sure you enjoyed that.

JAMIE. I really did.

MARY. Good for you.

> *(She sighs. Then makes herself a small cup of coffee.)*

JAMIE. I hope you're gonna pay for that.

MARY. Right.

JAMIE. Seriously, no special treatment for employees.

MARY. Yeah, I've noticed.

JAMIE. Seriously, Brad's got cameras everywhere, he's probably taking notes on us all the time.

MARY. Well, that's really creepy.

JAMIE. Yup.

MARY. Well – whatever, you can deduct thirty-seven cents from my paycheck if it makes you feel better.

JAMIE. It doesn't.

MARY. Okay, well – sorry. What is your problem today?

JAMIE. Nothing.

MARY. You're in a weird mood.

JAMIE. No I'm not.

MARY. You kind of are.

JAMIE. No, I'm just being my charming self.

MARY. ...Okay, well, it's not that charming, actually.

JAMIE. Yeahhh I know.

> *(She pulls a book from under the counter and flips through to find her place. JAMIE nods and looks down at his hands.)*

Rufus said, um – that Danny took your car somewhere?

MARY. Oh – Yeah – So – he got a job.

JAMIE. Oh, no shit!

MARY. Yeah, it just happened last night.

JAMIE. That's awesome.

MARY. Yeah. It's really really good.

JAMIE. Tell him congrats for me, that's so / awesome.

MARY. Yeah, I will, he's... I feel like he's about to turn a corner or / something.

JAMIE. Yeah, good. What is it?

MARY. This electrician in Scranton. He's got this huge job, I guess, so he hired Danny to help / out.

JAMIE. Okay.

MARY. But he says if it goes okay, then he'll just keep him on as like a regular.

JAMIE. That's awesome.

MARY. I know. Something's finally happening, you know?

JAMIE. Yeah, totally. Is that why he needed your car – to go to work?

MARY. Yeah. Well, to go meet with the guy.

JAMIE. Oh, nice.

MARY. Rufus was really nice to drive me home.

JAMIE. Yeah, he...said he drove you home.

MARY. Yeah.

> *(A pause. She tears at a hangnail. He watches her. Then shakes his head.)*

...What?

JAMIE. Nothing.

MARY. What?

JAMIE. Nothing, he just – I mean... I guess I always think things will change or be better between us, or he'll decide to suddenly be less of a dick, but then – that never happens, so – that kind of sucks. And they're too much drama for me.

MARY. Drama?

JAMIE. Yeah, I don't know, they're / just –

MARY. Oh no.

JAMIE. Yeah. It's – complicated, I guess. I don't know.

MARY. Yeah, Rufus said, um – They're just fighting a lot or something?

JAMIE. No – I shouldn't have said anything.

MARY. She seems kind of intense.

JAMIE. Yeah, I don't know. I think she's pretty badass, actually, but –

> *(He shrugs.)*

So you and Rufus are like best friends now?

MARY. God – Um, not really.

JAMIE. Okay.

MARY. I mean... I really like him. I always liked him. We just
– I don't know, I think we're really similar, actually...
like I can talk to him. About the world. At large. So.
That's nice.

> (JAMIE *looks at his hands, nodding his head.*)
>
> (RUFUS *and* PETA *appear outside;* RUFUS
> *knocks on the glass.*)

JAMIE. Well – Shit – Speaking of.

RUFUS. Hey.

> (RUFUS *and* PETA *step inside.* MARY *smooths
> her hair and cleans a spot on the counter.*)

JAMIE. You're up early.

RUFUS. I know, / we –

JAMIE. Well, earlier than two p.m., so that's pretty good.

RUFUS. Yes, I'm – I know, I'm turning over a new leaf –
um, no – we, uh – wanted to come by and say a proper
goodbye.

JAMIE. Oh – you're heading out?

RUFUS. Yeah, we gotta get back to the city, so...you can have
your house back now.

JAMIE. Oh – / no worries.

PETA. Thank you for having us.

JAMIE. You don't have to thank / me, god.

PETA. It was very kind of you.

JAMIE. Well, thanks. It was my pleasure.

> (*She hugs him tightly.*)

Whoa.

PETA. Thank you.

JAMIE. You're welcome.

PETA. Is it all right if I use your bathroom really quick?

JAMIE. Oh, yeah – right over there.

PETA. Thanks.

(She squeezes his arm, glances over at **MARY**, *and heads to the bathroom.)*

Hi Mary, how are you?

MARY. Hey – good.

*(***PETA*** gives a tight smile and disappears.* ***JAMIE*** and ***RUFUS*** stand together, quiet for a moment.* ***MARY*** stares at the bakery case.)*

JAMIE. So, uh...drive safely.

RUFUS. Yeah – oh thanks – we will. I, uh...

(He glances up. **MARY** *exits into the back room.)*

Um – hey, so I know we descended on you with a lot of – stuff, so.

JAMIE. S'okay.

RUFUS. Sorry about that.

JAMIE. Well, it's – you know. I don't know.

RUFUS. What.

JAMIE. Well, it just feels really shitty.

RUFUS. Okay.

JAMIE. I mean this is a shitty way to leave everything, I guess is what I mean.

RUFUS. I know, I just – I'm – wading through a lot of shit right now.

*(***JAMIE*** nods, quiet.)*

I mean I've got – *her* – and work and I'm... I kind of have to leave things a little shitty while I go home and backtrack and make other things less shitty first.

*(***JAMIE*** nods.)*

JAMIE. Well. Good luck, I guess.

RUFUS. Yeah, thank you – I will need it!

(He shakes his head and laughs to himself.)

Um, so, yeah – I think you made a pretty accurate assessment.

JAMIE. What?

RUFUS. That unfortunately I have become our father's son, so...

JAMIE. Eh, well you're not *that* bad...

>   (**RUFUS** *laughs.*)

Well, pretty sure you made the right assessment on me too, so.

RUFUS. No, that was...

JAMIE. *(Shrugging.)* Eh. You did.

>   (*He looks up at his brother. Then points his head at the bathroom.*)

...So, what are you guys going to...?

RUFUS. Uhhhh I don't really know.

JAMIE. Okay.

RUFUS. Sooo...we'll see! Not looking good.

JAMIE. That's too bad.

RUFUS. Yeah.

>   (*They both stare at their shoes.* **RUFUS** *smiles sadly.* **JAMIE** *nods.* **PETA** *emerges from the bathroom.*)

So! – Uhhh, anyway...we should get going.

JAMIE. Yeah, yeah.

RUFUS. Ready?

PETA. Yes.

>   (**MARY** *re-enters and busies herself cleaning a spot on the counter.*)

JAMIE. Well. Come back any time. Both of you.

RUFUS. Thanks, yeah, maybe in the summer or something.

JAMIE. Yeah, that'd be nice.

RUFUS. Cool. Well. Bye, man.

JAMIE. Bye.

>   (*They hug awkwardly.*)

PETA. It was so nice to meet you.

JAMIE. Oh, yeah – you too.

RUFUS. Bye Mary.

MARY. Oh – Bye.

RUFUS. Say bye to Danny for me.

MARY. I will.

RUFUS. And, um...good luck with everything.

MARY. Yeah – you too.

    If I'm, um –

RUFUS. *(Turning back.)* Sorry?

MARY. I might make it to the city, so – I'll let you know.

RUFUS. Oh – yeah... Well, Jamie has my email, so.

MARY. Okay.

RUFUS. Bye guys.

> *(**RUFUS** nods and turns away. He and **PETA** leave. **JAMIE** stares after him. **JAMIE** holds his hand up to wave as they drive away.)*
>
> *(**MARY** studies the spot on the counter, silent for a long moment.)*

MARY. Gonna feed the cats.

JAMIE. Okay.

> *(He watches her as she grabs the bag of cat food hidden under a shelf, stalks into the back, and disappears.)*

7. Behind The Bakery

(One and a half weeks later, early morning.
MARY *stands behind the bakery, smoking, her*
eyes closed. It's quiet and cold out; she doesn't
wear a coat.)

*(**JAMIE** opens the back door and peers at her.)*

JAMIE. ...You're smoking?

MARY. Yup.

JAMIE. Already?

MARY. Yes.

JAMIE. Bad morning?

> *(She doesn't answer. He steps outside.)*

God – It's freezing / out here.

MARY. I know.

JAMIE. You don't wear coats / anymore?

MARY. Jamie I'm on my break.

JAMIE. We open in like / ten minutes.

MARY. I know I'm taking my break before everyone starts
screaming at me about what kind of bran muffin they
want.

JAMIE. There's pretty much just the / one kind.

MARY. Jamie.

JAMIE. Okay, sorry.

> *(He stares at his breath.)*

You okay?

MARY. Yup.

JAMIE. You look tired.

MARY. Jamie, don't tell a woman she looks tired.

JAMIE. I didn't mean it / like that.

MARY. It's insulting.

JAMIE. I'm sorry.

MARY. Just – keep that in your head as a good lesson to go
by in life.

JAMIE. Thanks.

(They both stare at their breath.)

Haven't seen the cats around in a couple days.

MARY. I know – I'm worried.

JAMIE. Yeah, they're fine, though.

MARY. That little grey one is so little.

JAMIE. He's – don't worry. They're like little ninjas. Did you see the big orange guy scale the fence / that time?

MARY. It's too cold for them.

JAMIE. They're cats.

MARY. I know that.

JAMIE. They're wearing little fur coats.

MARY. I know.

JAMIE. You worry too much.

MARY. Yeah, well – There are things to worry about.

JAMIE. I know.

MARY. So.

JAMIE. So –

D'you watch the hockey game?

(She shoots him a look.)

Total upset. Augh, it was amazing actually – like I've never seen Brodeur* like that, and I've seen him like on fire and blocking everything in sight, but not like, I mean it was INSANE, / just...

MARY. Yeah, I – can I just be alone for the next three minutes that I have?

*(**JAMIE** looks at her. A pause.)*

JAMIE. No.

MARY. What?

JAMIE. No. You can't.

What the hell is going on with you?

---

*Author's Note: At the time this play was written, Martin Brodeur was goalkeeper for Team USA in the Winter Games. His name should be replaced by a current goalkeeper who plays for the American team.

MARY. I just want to be by myself for a / few minutes –

JAMIE. No, I'm – it's just, what is so horrible that you have to shut down and not want to talk to anyone who clearly cares a lot about you or or wear a stupid coat when it's negative degrees out, I just – I don't get that. I don't get it.

MARY. Well we're different people, Jamie.

JAMIE. So you can't talk to me?

MARY. Just, no –

JAMIE. I want to know what's going on with / you.

MARY. Jamie.

JAMIE. Just TALK to me – Please Talk to Me.

(She is surprised by him.)

MARY. Danny...had an attack yesterday.

JAMIE. What's – what happened?

MARY. Uhhh, well... He's been working for that electrician for the last week, and it had been going really well, but then yesterday, I guess they were up in this attic or something and Danny just – freaked out.

JAMIE. Like...what...

MARY. Like apparently his vision went totally black and he – panicked and started screaming that he couldn't see and then basically fell apart.

JAMIE. Shit.

MARY. So they took him to the hospital. And I'm running over there thinking something awful happened, like he fell off a ladder or...got electrocuted or something, and I show up and the head electrician guy is there looking all embarrassed or something and the doctors are like, well, there's nothing wrong with him.

JAMIE. So his vision came back?

MARY. Yeah, he's fine now.

JAMIE. Well that's good at least.

MARY. Yeah, it's, I mean he's not *fine*... They gave him this pretty intense anti-anxiety thing which basically made him pass out as soon as we got home and then I just stayed up and watched stupid – figure skating all night.

JAMIE. Ah.

MARY. So that is why I'm tired, thanks for noticing by the way.

JAMIE. I'm sorry.

MARY. He really needed that job.

JAMIE. Yeah.

MARY. I really needed him to have that job, I – I actually started thinking he'd be okay and things would maybe be almost normal and maybe I would get to – have my life.

JAMIE. Yeah.

MARY. Anyway. We should get in there, right?

> (*She puts out her cigarette.* **JAMIE** *doesn't move.*)

JAMIE. What happened on figure skating?

MARY. Nothing.

JAMIE. I'm not fucking with you.

> (*She peers at him.*)

MARY. I... Well, it sucked. That's what happened.

JAMIE. Why?

MARY. Because it was the worst thing ever.

JAMIE. Why?

MARY. Because. Aughh – because. It was like the final final for the women's singles competition, right?

JAMIE. Yeah.

MARY. So there's this skater from Estonia. And. Well. She's amazing. Like her short program was killer, and so... basically everyone's looking to her, you know, because she's like come up from the bottom, like Estonia's never won a medal in this category or even this sport ever, so she'd be making big-time history.

JAMIE. Wow.

MARY. Yeah. AND her husband has just died.

JAMIE. Oh god.

MARY. I know. So she's skating *anyway*, despite this horrible thing that's happened like a few *weeks* before – she just has to nail her long program and she's got the gold.

JAMIE. So...

MARY. So – okay, so the music starts, right? And the entire place is like dead quiet. Like the air in the place is so taut, you can just feel it...like tightening around her. And then, like, she lifts her head and starts moving. And it's lovely and it's light and just the most graceful but also the most like – full thing you've ever seen, like every single movement is full of this this like incredible energy and presence, and they keep flashing the camera into the stands where her parents are sitting, and her dad's really frail-looking and like all stoic and Eastern-European-looking, but you can tell he's like beaming underneath – and so she's going and she's going and it's beautiful, like even the commentators are silent, and she nails the double axel and then she nails the triple axel and then another triple axel her mom has her arms up in the air, like victory, like – *(She demonstrates.)* and then she goes for the last triple axel, with this like incredible force – and she screws up the landing.

JAMIE. *(Quiet.)* Oh no.

MARY. She doesn't fall – she just loses her balance for one tiny moment, like she tips forward and has to catch herself with her hand. And the crowd like gasps and her dad closes his eyes and and...like time freezes... and then she rights herself and moves on to finish the program. So she throws herself into the final pose... and everyone's cheering and her parents are holding each other and her arms are in their pose but you can just – You can see something break in her – it's like this little crack running down the side of a teacup, just this terrible sense of failure like running across her skin. And she's thinking, I missed it. I missed it.

JAMIE. Wow.

MARY. Yeah. So.

JAMIE. Geez.

MARY. I couldn't sleep at ALL after that.

JAMIE. Yeah.

MARY. Just like, the WORST possible thing I could have watched, it was like – like a really fucked up joke.

> *(She stares at her feet, then looks up at him.)*

I'm worried that...

> *(She laughs/cries.)*

...And I guess I'm going to cry...

JAMIE. Hey.

MARY. I'm worried that this is all I get. You know – I'm really –...

> *(She cries. **JAMIE** steps toward her and then holds her. She collapses into him. They stand like this for a long moment. Then she pulls away and wipes her face, shy.)*

(Whispering.) Augh, shit.

JAMIE. I built a hotel.

MARY. *(Looking up.)* What?

JAMIE. For the cats. See – *(He points.)* it's over there – I kind of tucked it into that little space between the dumpster and the fence.

MARY. Oh my god.

JAMIE. It's like a double-decker-type thing – I lined it with straw. Which should apparently keep them pretty warm.

MARY. Jamie.

JAMIE. And there's a little thing attached to put their food in – I checked on them when I got in this morning. The big orange one was asleep on the first floor. The tabby was up top with the little grey guy.

MARY. Oh my god...

JAMIE. I was worried about them. It's fucking freezing out here.

MARY. I know.

JAMIE. So. Yeahhh.

We're not all that different.

MARY. ...No.

(They watch their breath, quiet for a moment.)

JAMIE. Okay, so... I have to go open the doors for the angry mob.

MARY. Okay.

JAMIE. But. You can stay out here.

MARY. Um...no. I'm coming.

JAMIE. Okay.

(He nods and heads inside, holding the door open for her. After a moment, she follows him.)

End of Play